D0032611

the **BAD GUYS**

in

THE FURBALL
STRIKES BACK

IF YOU PURCHASED THIS BOOK WITHOUT A COVER, YOU SHOULD BE AWARE THAT THIS BOOK IS STOLEN PROPERTY.
IT WAS REPORTED AS "UNSOLD AND DESTROYED" TO THE PUBLISHER, AND NEITHER THE AUTHOR NOR THE
PUBLISHER HAS RECEIVED ANY PAYMENT FOR THIS "STRIPPED BOOK."

TEXT AND ILLUSTRATIONS COPYRIGHT © 2016 BY AARON BLABEY

ALL RIGHTS RESERVED. PUBLISHED BY SCHOLASTIC INC., PUBLISHERS SINCE 1920. 557 BROADWAY,
NEW YORK, NY 10012. SCHOLASTIC AND ASSOCIATED LOGOS ARE TRADEMARKS AND/OR REGISTERED TRADEMARKS
OF SCHOLASTIC INC. THIS EDITION PUBLISHED UNDER LICENSE FROM SCHOLASTIC AUSTRALIA PTY LIMITED.
FIRST PUBLISHED BY SCHOLASTIC AUSTRALIA PTY LIMITED IN 2016.

THE PUBLISHER DOES NOT HAVE ANY CONTROL OVER AND DOES NOT ASSUME ANY
RESPONSIBILITY FOR AUTHOR OR THIRD-PARTY WEBSITES OR THEIR CONTENT.

NO PART OF THIS PUBLICATION MAY BE REPRODUCED, STORED IN A RETRIEVAL SYSTEM, OR TRANSMITTED IN ANY
FORM OR BY ANY MEANS, ELECTRONIC, MECHANICAL, PHOTOCOPYING, RECORDING, OR OTHERWISE, WITHOUT WRITTEN
PERMISSION OF THE PUBLISHER. FOR INFORMATION REGARDING PERMISSION, WRITE TO SCHOLASTIC AUSTRALIA, AN
IMPRINT OF SCHOLASTIC AUSTRALIA PTY LIMITED, 345 PACIFIC HIGHWAY, LINDFIELD NSW 2070 AUSTRALIA.

THIS BOOK IS A WORK OF FICTION. NAMES, CHARACTERS, PLACES, AND INCIDENTS ARE EITHER THE PRODUCT
OF THE AUTHOR'S IMAGINATION OR ARE USED FICTITIOUSLY, AND ANY RESEMBLANCE TO ACTUAL PERSONS,
LIVING OR DEAD, BUSINESS ESTABLISHMENTS, EVENTS, OR LOCALES IS ENTIRELY COINCIDENTAL.

LIBRARY OF CONGRESS CATALOGING-IN-PUBLICATION DATA AVAILABLE

ISBN 978-1-358-08749-9

10 9 8 7   17 18 19 20

PRINTED IN THE U.S.A.   23
FIRST U.S. PRINTING 2016

· AARON BLABEY ·

the BAD GUYS

WITHDRAWN

in

SCHOLASTIC INC.

THE FURBALL
STRIKES BACK

HEROES OR VILLAINS?

A SPECIAL REPORT BY

TIFFANY FLUFFIT 6 NEWS

1

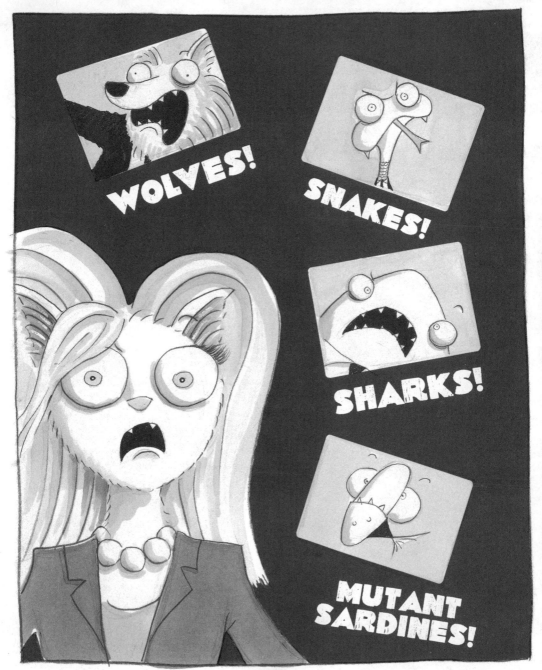

WOLVES!

SNAKES!

SHARKS!

MUTANT SARDINES!

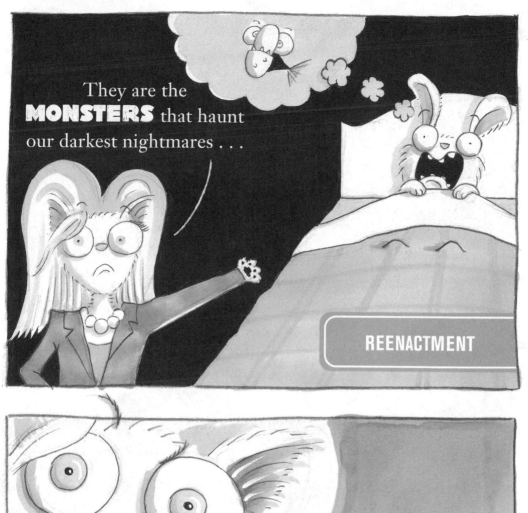

They are the **MONSTERS** that haunt our darkest nightmares . . .

REENACTMENT

Or ARE they?

Well, not according to THIS chicken . . .

SUNNYSIDE CHICKEN FARM was a terrible place. We spent our whole lives locked in tiny cages. But then that wonderful wolf and his friends—they set us free!

BROOKE

But . . . didn't one of them try to EAT you?

Yes. But he spat me back out again.

IS THIS CHICKEN *CRAZY?*

And Brooke is not the only one to claim that these VILLAINS are actually . . .

HEROES IN DISGUISE!

Every one of the 10,000 chickens set free from Sunnyside has told the same story.

POLICE
REPORT

Sunnyside

SHOULD MUTANT SARDINES BE ALLOWED TO WALK THE STREETS?

I thought they were lovely.
Especially the really big chicken.
Or maybe he was a shark.
It was hard to tell . . .

PAT, HOMEMAKER

They inspired me to
follow my dreams.
I'll never forget them.

FIONA, CELEBRITY CHEF

We should all be careful not to judge
others simply by the way they *look*.
Sometimes the scariest-looking creatures
can be the kindest and best of all.

DIANE, SUPREME COURT JUDGE

So, can ALL these chickens be **CRAZY?**

Or are those

HORRIFYING CREATURES

actually . . . trying to do good?

Are they out there doing good deeds?

Or are they **LURKING OUTSIDE YOUR DOOR**, waiting for a chance to show us that they're nothing but a bunch of . . .

... BAD GUYS?!

· CHAPTER 1 ·

IF YOU GO DOWN TO THE WOODS TODAY...

Great! So, let's go over the plan ONE MORE TIME.

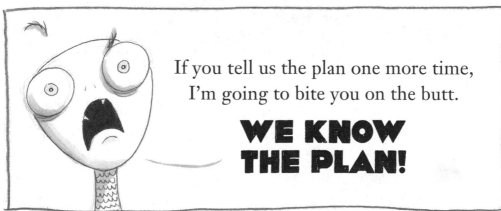

If you tell us the plan one more time, I'm going to bite you on the butt.

WE KNOW THE PLAN!

Hey! Take it easy, Mr. Snake. This is important.

So anyway . . . I got an **ANONYMOUS CALL** telling me that way out here in **THE WOODS**, there's a bunch of **BULLDOZERS** getting ready to smash up the homes of a lot of **CUTE, FURRY ANIMALS**.

And we're here to make sure

THAT DOESN'T HAPPEN.

WE KNOW ALREADY!

Oh man . . . I don't feel good AT ALL . . .

MR. SHARK!

What?

Where's your disguise?

Oh yeah.
I forgot.

See?! **THIS** is why I
keep repeating the plan!

Yeah, yeah.
Whatevs.

Hey! Who's
THAT guy?!

Relax. It's just me.

You are SO good at disguises.

Yeah. I know.

Now, remember, Shark—YOU are a
CUTE FURRY ANIMAL!
It's your job to distract the guys
driving the bulldozers while we—

WE KNOW THE PLAN!

Uh-oh. Stop the car . . .

WE'VE BEEN OVER IT A **MILLION** TIMES AND WE **KNOW THE PLAN!**

STOP THE CAR!

SCREEECH!

What's wrong?!

Where are YOU going?

I need to go "number two."

You need to *WHAT*?!

Car travel upsets my tummy.

Are you serious?!
The bulldozers are
**RIGHT
THERE!**

Start without me.
I shouldn't be too long.

Well . . . if you've gotta go . . .

UNBELIEVABLE.

Let's just do it.
He'll catch up.

Yeah, man.
I'm ready.

LEGS

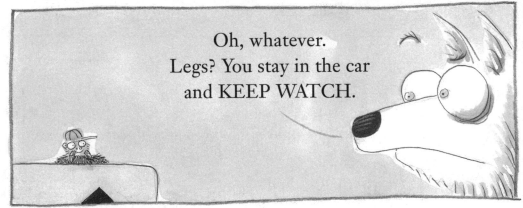

Oh, whatever.
Legs? You stay in the car
and KEEP WATCH.

You got it.
If anything moves within
1,000 yards, I'll see it.

All right.
It's time to
be HEROES.

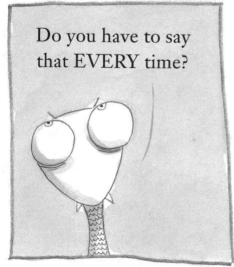

Do you have to say
that EVERY time?

LET'S
ROCK!

Um . . . guys . . . ?

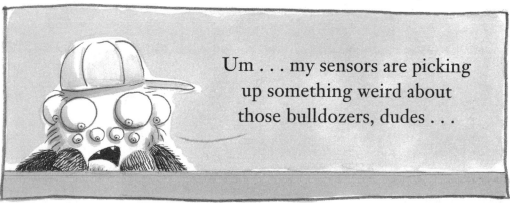

Um . . . my sensors are picking up something weird about those bulldozers, dudes . . .

Um . . .

My car!

LEGS!

Hey, does anyone else think the ground feels weird?

AAARRGGHH!!!

· CHAPTER 2 ·
the LAIR OF
DR. MARMALADE

Wha . . . ?

Well, HELLO, genius.
Nice of you to join us . . .

We're tied up!

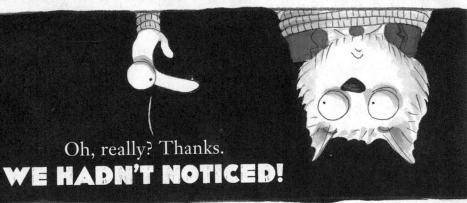

Oh, really? Thanks.
WE HADN'T NOTICED!

But who would do this?

Who *wouldn't* do this?
We're **BAD** guys, man.
Guys like us don't get a
happy ending.

NO!

There must have
been a mistake!
**WE'RE
HEROES!**

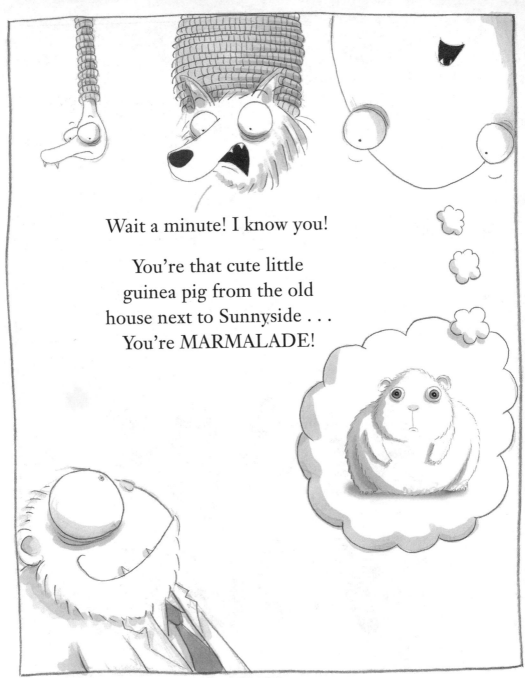

Wait a minute! I know you!

You're that cute little
guinea pig from the old
house next to Sunnyside . . .
You're MARMALADE!

That's **DOCTOR**
Marmalade to you!

Forgive me.

Allow me to
introduce myself . . .

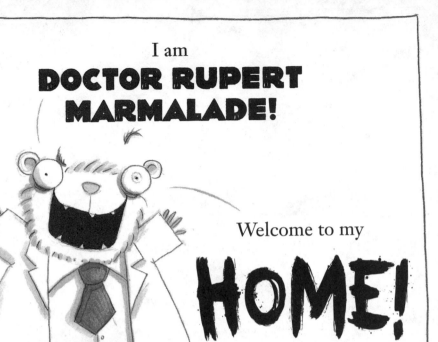

I am
DOCTOR RUPERT MARMALADE!

Welcome to my

HOME!

Hey! I've heard of you!
You're that
BILLIONAIRE MAD SCIENTIST.

Billionaire mad scientist?!
He's a **GUINEA PIG!**

So what?! Just because I'm a guinea pig, I CAN'T BE A

BILLIONAIRE MAD SCIENTIST?

Oh. Well, no . . . I suppose you could be . . .

Yeah, that's right! And you blew up my awesome car. Why would you do that if you weren't **CRAZY?**

Well, let me think.

Hmmm, yes. Tell me . . . Did you think you could just **BREAK INTO** one of my **CHICKEN FARMS** and steal **10,000 CHICKENS** and I'd just be **COOL WITH THAT?!**

YOUR chicken farm?
But you're just a guinea pig!

YOU'RE STILL NOT GETTING IT—
I'M A BILLIONAIRE MAD SCIENTIST WHO **OWNS A LOT OF CHICKEN FARMS** AND I'M VERY ANGRY WITH YOU!

Hang on. Are you saying that you blew up our car and strung us up **JUST** because we rescued those chickens?

FINALLY!
Yes, that's right.

But you're *not* mad about all the **BAD** stuff we've done in our lives?

No.

So that means . . .

THE ONLY REASON WE'RE IN THIS MESS IS BECAUSE OF YOUR STUPID OBSESSION WITH **BEING A HERO!**

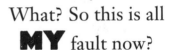

What? So this is all **MY** fault now?

OF COURSE IT IS! THE ONLY REASON THIS **CRAZY** GUINEA PIG HAS TIED US UP IS BECAUSE YOU **KEEP MAKING US DO GOOD!**

You really want to fight about this NOW?

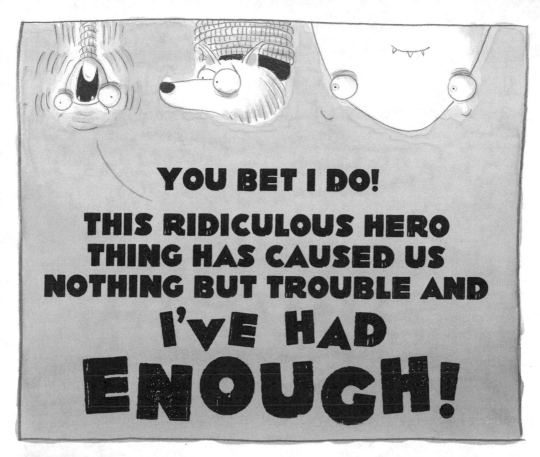

YOU BET I DO!

THIS RIDICULOUS HERO THING HAS CAUSED US NOTHING BUT TROUBLE AND

I'VE HAD

ENOUGH!

Hey!

WHAT?!

I think you have failed to notice my beautiful new toy. Isn't it LOVELY?

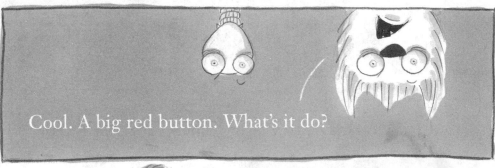

Cool. A big red button. What's it do?

Oh, nothing much . . .

· CHAPTER 3 ·
DO YOU SEE WHAT I SEE?

Hey! *Chicos!*
Where is everybody?
It's not my fault I
needed to poop!

VOOMP!

Shhh!

¡Ay, caramba! What happened to you?!

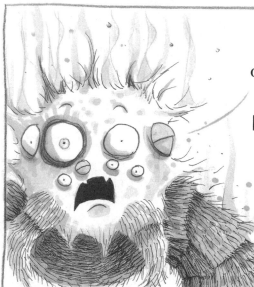

I jumped from the car one millisecond before it was **BLOWN TO PIECES BY A LASER CANNON** and then I watched the rest of the gang get **SUCKED INTO THE BOWELS OF THE EARTH.**

Oh. Cool.

WHAT?!

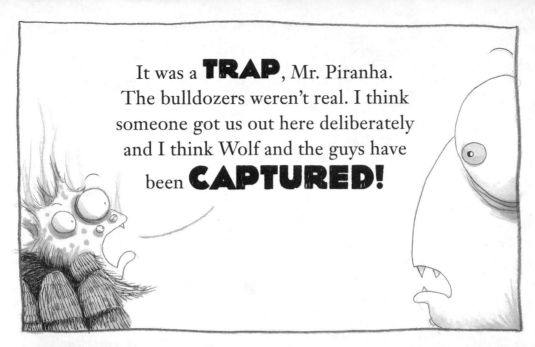

It was a **TRAP**, Mr. Piranha. The bulldozers weren't real. I think someone got us out here deliberately and I think Wolf and the guys have been **CAPTURED!**

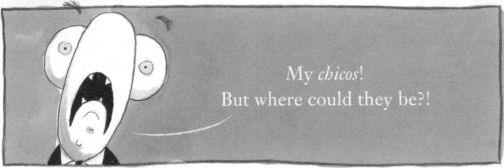

My *chicos*! But where could they be?!

Look over there . . .

Sunnyside?!
But what's a chicken farm doing out
here in the middle of the woods?

Exactly!
Fishy, don't you think?

Hey! Who are you calling "Fishy"?
And yes, I DO think.

Um . . . OK. Anyway . . .
We need to get inside that
building, and I have a plan . . .

Give us a kiss.

FAINT!

Wow. He's out cold. You really do freak everyone out, don't you?

Yep. Always have . . .

. . . always . . . will . . .

Hey!

What?

I think . . . I just saw . . .

...a **NINJA!**

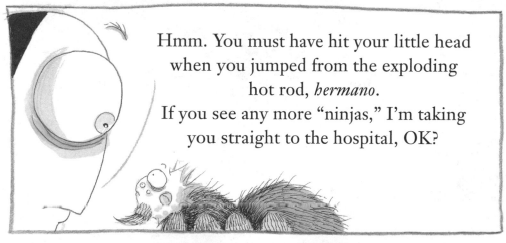

Hmm. You must have hit your little head when you jumped from the exploding hot rod, *hermano*.
If you see any more "ninjas," I'm taking you straight to the hospital, OK?

Because I don't know what we'll find in here, *chico*. But I'll promise you one thing . . .

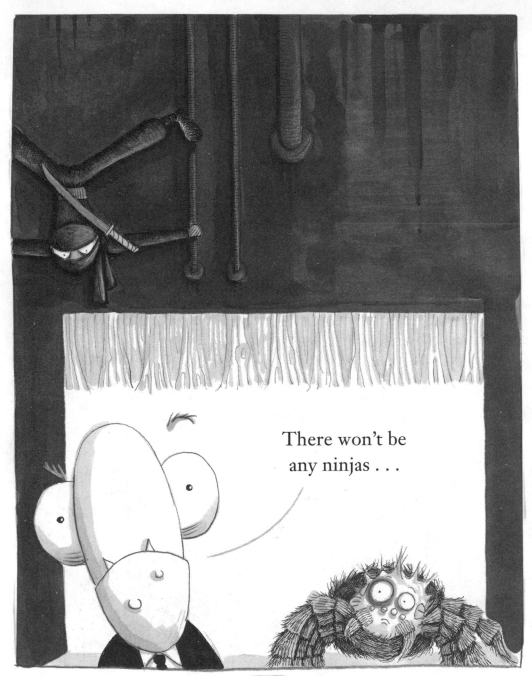

· CHAPTER 4 ·
the MIND OF A MONSTER

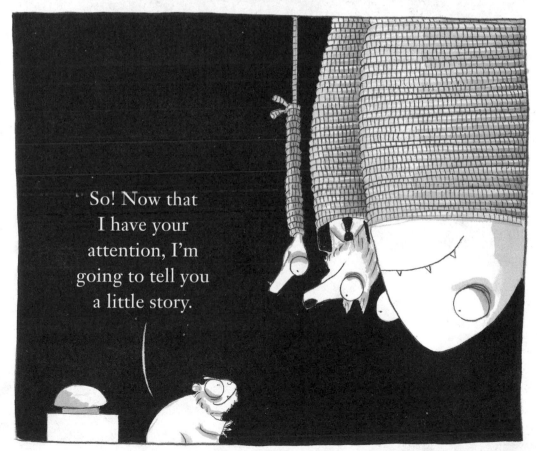

So! Now that I have your attention, I'm going to tell you a little story.

Once upon a time,
there was an itty, bitty guinea pig who got

SICK

of everyone saying how
CUTE and **CUDDLY** he was.

So he decided to do something about it . . .

First of all, he made billions of dollars putting chickens in cages, but somehow that just wasn't enough.

SO! He created a **SECRET WEAPON** that would make sure **NO ONE EVER** called him **CUTE** and **CUDDLY** again. A weapon **SO POWERFUL** that it would change the world forever with the push of a button . . .

THIS BUTTON!

But what's wrong with being
cute and cuddly?
I wish *I* were cute and cuddly!
Everyone **LOVES** guinea pigs.

I don't want *love*,
you ridiculous fish.

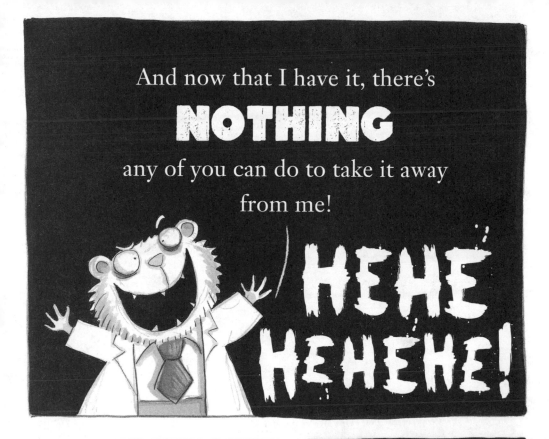

And now that I have it, there's

NOTHING

any of you can do to take it away
from me!

HEHE HEHEHE!

Ahhh . . . sorry. Can you
just give us a second?

What?
Um . . . all right.
But don't take long, OK?

OK. So the guinea pig is out of his mind. What do we do?

You tell us, fur-brain. What's your next big idea?

Listen, Snake, you'd better start helping out here or—

OR WHAT?

Guys, cut it out.

OR YOU'LL BE **SORRY**,
YOU NASTY LITTLE
OVERGROWN SLUG!

OH, *REALLY*?

AND WHAT ARE YOU GOING TO DO?

ARE YOU GOING TO

BORE ME TO DEATH

WITH YOUR NEXT IDIOTIC PLAN TO TURN US ALL INTO **GOODY-GOODY GUMDROPS?!**

THAT'S YOUR LAST WARNING, SNAKE.

You both need to stop arguing. It's starting to really UPSET me . . .

Warning, schmorning! Do your worst, you dimwitted **HERO WANNABE!**

THAT'S IT!

DON'T DO IT, WOLF.

TOO LATE!

MUNCH!

And you just ate the wolf!

Shark! What do you think you're doing?! Spit me out!

NO.

NOT UNTIL YOU
CAN BOTH LEARN
TO BE FRIENDS.

I'm warning you, Wolf! Cough me up!

Not a chance, Slimy.
Shark! I'm NOT going to ask you again!

Wait a minute! Are you inside the shark?!

None of your business!

But that means I'm inside a wolf AND a shark!

Tell someone who cares!

This is like being trapped inside some kind of really disgusting nesting doll and I DON'T LIKE IT!

Big whoop.
Shark, I'm going to count to ten . . .

You wouldn't
BELIEVE
what I have to put up with.

• CHAPTER 5 •
SURPRISE, SURPRISE

Oh, man! There are guards everywhere!
How are we ever going to find them?

Hey, look!
Down there!

It's Shark!

NO ONE TIES UP MY *CHICOS* AND GETS AWAY WITH IT! LET'S CUT THAT ROPE **RIGHT NOW!**

NIBBLE!

NIBBLE!
NIBBLE!

Mr. Piranha?

Yeah, kid? What is it?

NIBBLE!
NIBBLE!

I know this sounds crazy . . .
but I really do think
I saw a ninja.

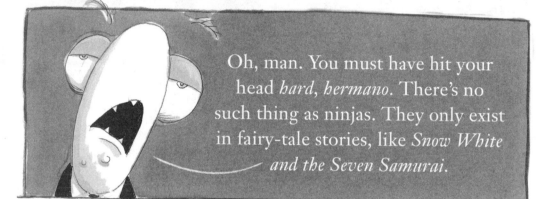

Oh, man. You must have hit your head *hard*, *hermano*. There's no such thing as ninjas. They only exist in fairy-tale stories, like *Snow White and the Seven Samurai*.

Actually, I'm pretty sure that's not true . . .

FREEZE!

Oh no!

SHARK! I'm sorry! They caught us!

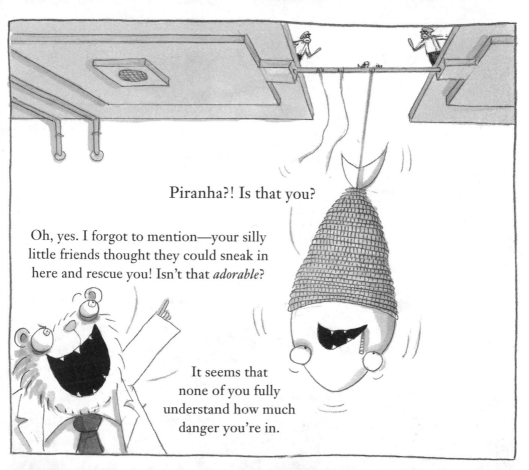

Piranha?! Is that you?

Oh, yes. I forgot to mention—your silly little friends thought they could sneak in here and rescue you! Isn't that *adorable*?

It seems that none of you fully understand how much danger you're in.

Oh well. I guess I'll just

UNLEASH THE END OF THE WORLD AS WE KNOW IT!

If you don't mind me saying, you seem like a very troubled guinea pig.

You have NO idea.

NOW LET'S GET THIS PARTY STARTED!

PIRANHA! RUN!

He cut the rope!

SPLURT!

Squeak!

OK. Does someone want to tell me what's going on here?

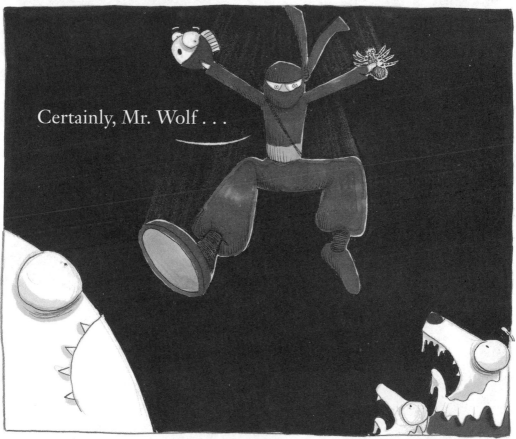

Certainly, Mr. Wolf . . .

LEGS! YOU'RE ALIVE!

FLING!

FLING!

So, tell me . . .

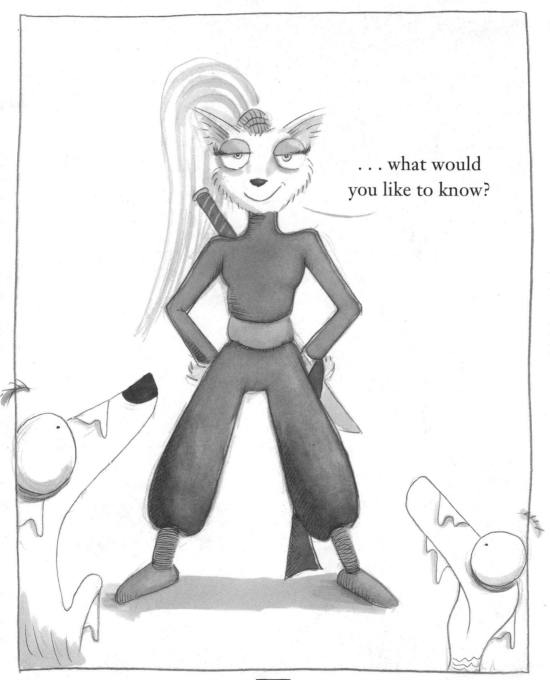

· CHAPTER 6 ·
the SECRET AGENT

Who **ARE** you?

My name is
**SPECIAL
AGENT FOX**,
Mr. Shark.
And I'm very pleased
to meet you.

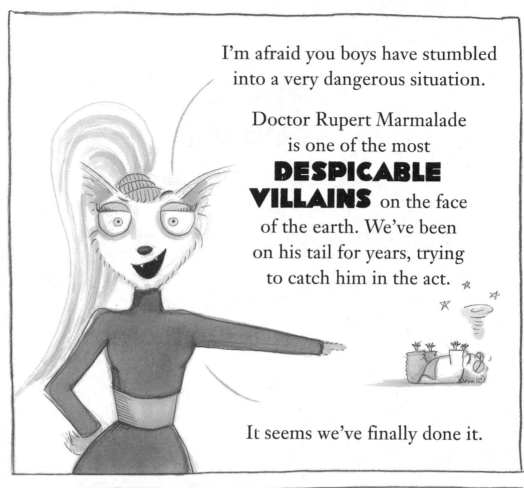

I'm afraid you boys have stumbled into a very dangerous situation.

Doctor Rupert Marmalade is one of the most **DESPICABLE VILLAINS** on the face of the earth. We've been on his tail for years, trying to catch him in the act.

It seems we've finally done it.

We? Who's *we*?

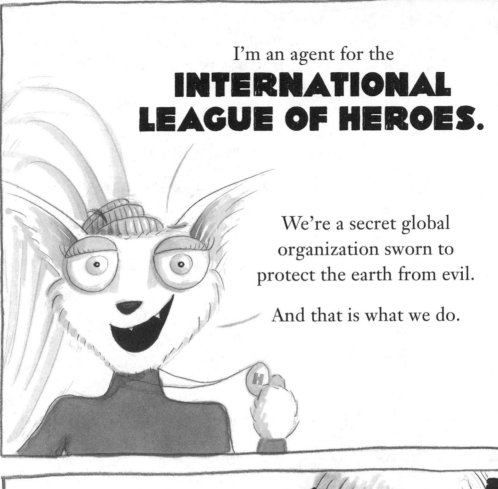

I'm an agent for the

INTERNATIONAL LEAGUE OF HEROES.

We're a secret global organization sworn to protect the earth from evil.

And that is what we do.

Hey! That's kind of what *we* do, isn't it, Wolfie?

Wolfie?

What's up with him?

. . . So awesome . . .
. . . so pretty . . .
. . . *guuuhhhhh* . . .
. . . *mhuuuunghhh* . . .

I'm not sure what's happening . . .

Never mind.

We are the . . .
Good Guys Club,
Agent Fox . . .
at your service . . .
heh heh heh . . .
ah . . . yup . . .
gughhhh . . .

The "Good
Guys Club"?
Is that what you
call yourselves?

Yep. We sat up ALL NIGHT
trying to think of the
STUPIDEST NAME in
the HISTORY OF **STUPID**
NAMES and—**BAM!**—
there it was.

Oh, I don't know.
I think it's kind of cute.

But I'm afraid you're a little
out of your depth here, boys.

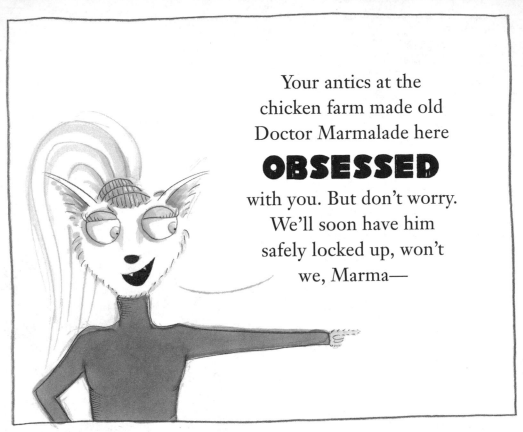

Your antics at the chicken farm made old Doctor Marmalade here

OBSESSED

with you. But don't worry. We'll soon have him safely locked up, won't we, Marma—

Oh dear.

Has anyone seen where the supervillain went?

Right here, Agent Fox.

Whoops. That's unfortunate.

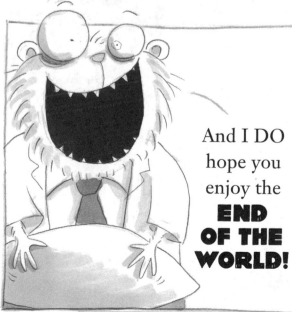

And I DO hope you enjoy the **END OF THE WORLD!**

He he!

CLUNK!

MY **SECRET WEAPON** HAS BEEN RELEASED AND IT'S **ON ITS WAY!** CAN YOU GUESS WHAT IT IS?

HEHE HE!

Oh, and just to make things a little more interesting . . .

FOOF!

THIS BUILDING WILL SELF-DESTRUCT IN 90 SECONDS . . .

89! 88! 87! 86!

76! 75! 74! 73!

Hmm. The old disappearing-up-a-great-big-bendy-tube trick. That's disappointing.

Well, the building is about to blow and we have seconds to live. Any ideas, gentlemen?

• CHAPTER 7 •
LEARNING TO RIDE A BIKE

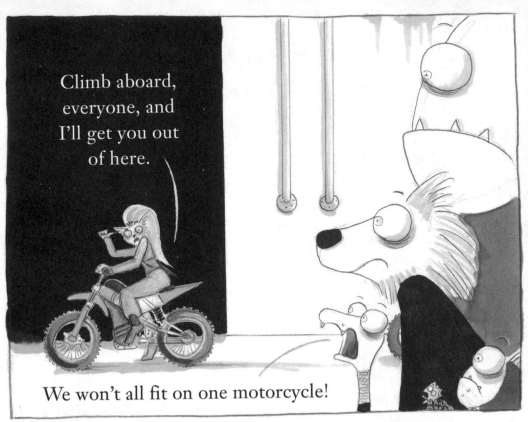

Climb aboard, everyone, and I'll get you out of here.

We won't all fit on one motorcycle!

Hmm. You could be right. I don't suppose any of you can ride one of these . . . ?

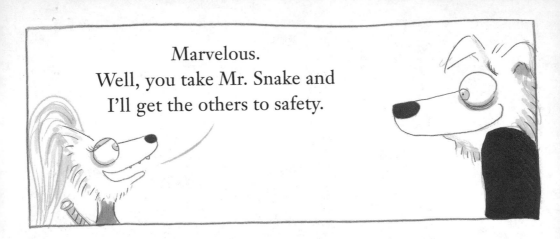

Marvelous.
Well, you take Mr. Snake and
I'll get the others to safety.

Good luck,
Mr. Wolf.

PECK!

I just didn't want to disappoint her.

You know what?

What?

Let's just . . .

PUT THE PEDAL TO THE METAL!

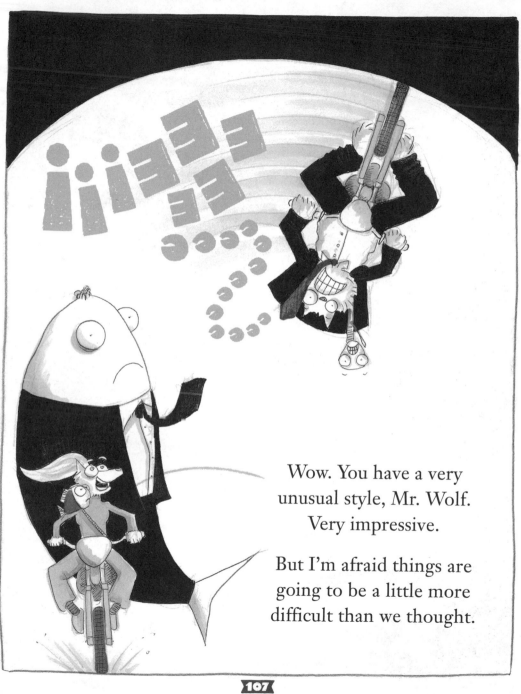

Wow. You have a very unusual style, Mr. Wolf. Very impressive.

But I'm afraid things are going to be a little more difficult than we thought.

Oh, really? Why's that?

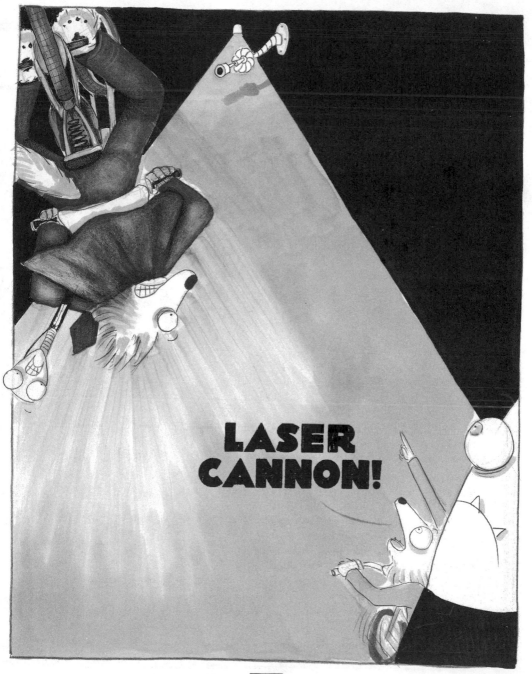

ZAP!

WOLF!
YOU'RE HEADING STRAIGHT FOR THE CANNON!

FIZZZBOOOOM!

IT'S NOT MY FAULT! I CAN'T RIDE A MOTORCYCLE!!

Wow. He really is awfully brave, isn't he?

Well, yes. In Bolivia, we have a name for people like that . . .

We call them "idiots."

I HATE YOU, WOLF!

WELL, I **DON'T** HATE YOU, SNAKE!

AND I **WON'T GIVE UP ON YOU**, NO MATTER WHAT HAPPENS.

I'M SORRY I **ATE** YOU EARLIER. BUT I'M **NOT** SORRY FOR GETTING YOU INTO ALL THIS TROUBLE.

THIS IS WHAT HEROES DO.

AND I TRULY BELIEVE **YOU HAVE A HERO INSIDE YOU**, MR. SNAKE.

AND I'LL NEVER STOP BELIEVING THAT. **EVER**.

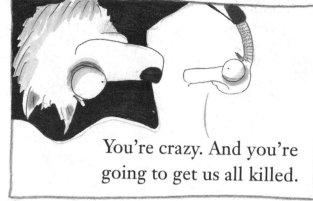

You're crazy. And you're going to get us all killed.

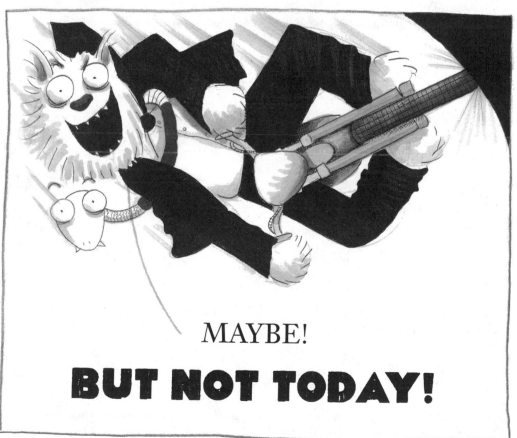

MAYBE!

BUT NOT TODAY!

THIS BUILDING WILL SELF-DESTRUCT IN 10 SECONDS . . . 9! 8! 7! 6! 5!

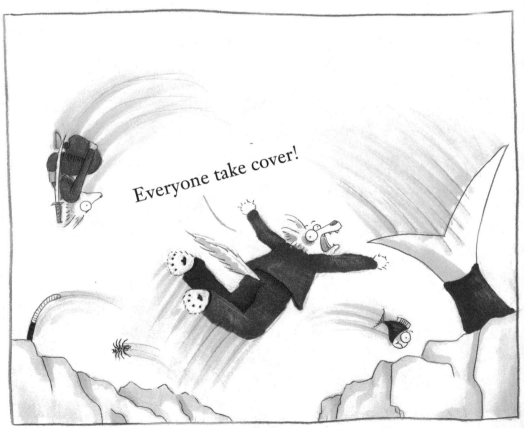

· CHAPTER 8 ·
A LITTLE FAVOR

What happened?
Did we blow up?
Is this . . . heaven?

It can't be.
You're here.

Tricked you!
The building wasn't
REALLY going to blow up!

Are you kidding?!
I nearly pooped my pants!

Again?!
You really need to
see a doctor, man.

YOU DIDN'T
REALLY THINK
I'D BLOW UP MY
**SECRET
WEAPON**,
DID YOU?

I'm getting sick of this.
WHAT secret weapon?
I'll bet it's just another trick!

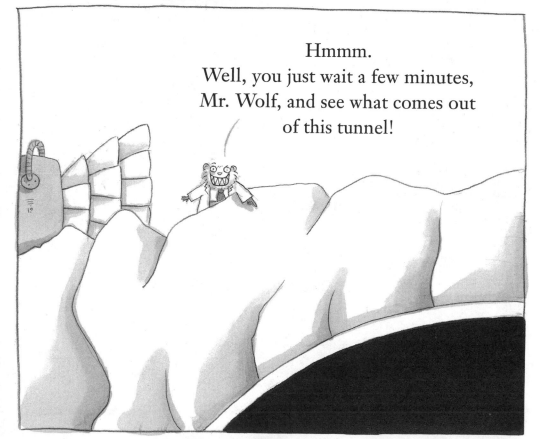

Hmmm.
Well, you just wait a few minutes,
Mr. Wolf, and see what comes out
of this tunnel!

YOU believe me, don't you, Agent Fox?

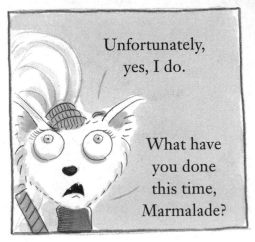

Unfortunately, yes, I do.

What have you done this time, Marmalade?

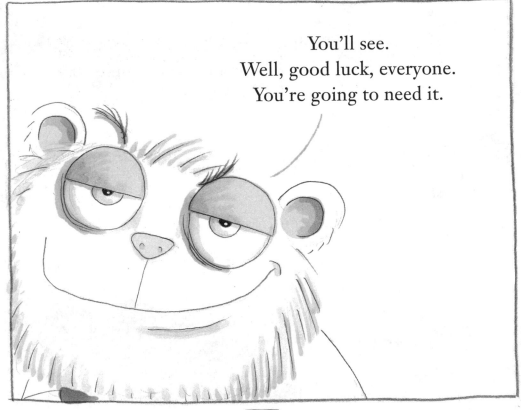

You'll see.
Well, good luck, everyone.
You're going to need it.

Nor do I, Mr. Wolf. And that's why I need to ask you a favor.

Anything!

I need to follow Marmalade **RIGHT NOW**. But someone needs to stay here and deal with his **SECRET WEAPON**.

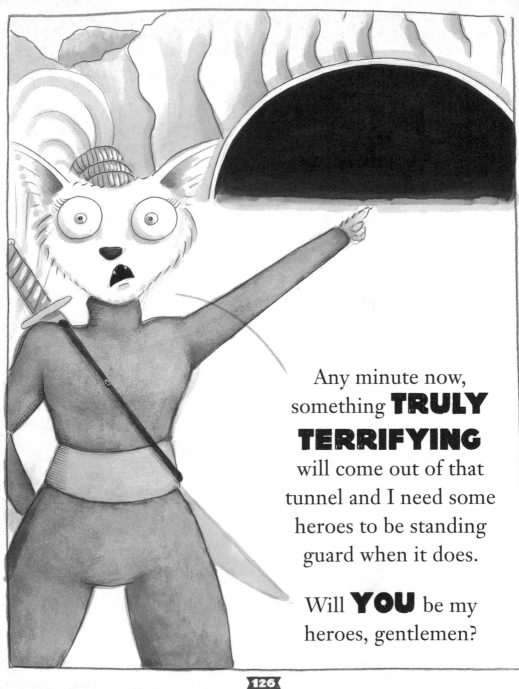

Any minute now, something **TRULY TERRIFYING** will come out of that tunnel and I need some heroes to be standing guard when it does.

Will **YOU** be my heroes, gentlemen?

Will you help me

SAVE THE WORLD?

Um . . . I'm really not sure . . .

I actually have a hair
appointment to get to . . .

I'd love to help, *señorita*, but I'm afraid
I need to find a clean pair of pants . . .

Sister, you're out of your mind . . .

127

OF COURSE WE WILL!

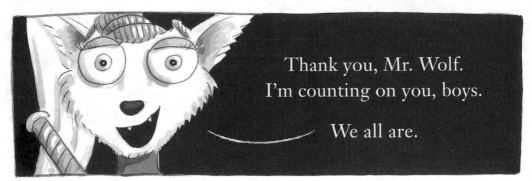

Thank you, Mr. Wolf.
I'm counting on you, boys.

We all are.

Oh great.
Now she's counting on us.

Yes, there are quite a few perks to being a hero, Mr. Wolf.

Oh, and Mr. Snake?

Yeah?

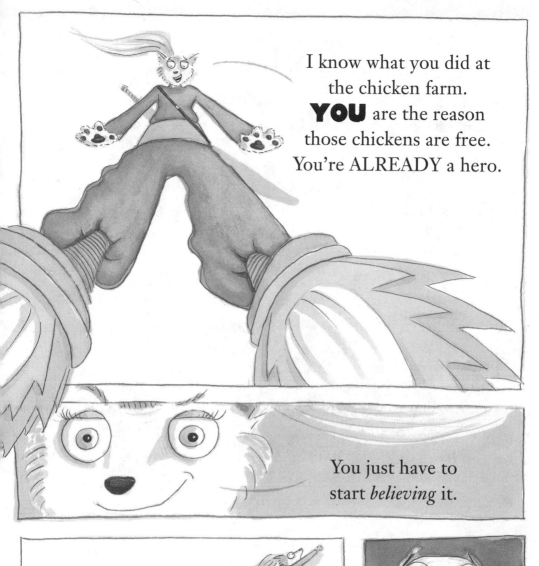

I know what you did at the chicken farm. **YOU** are the reason those chickens are free. You're ALREADY a hero.

You just have to start *believing* it.

Good luck, boys!

ZOOOOM!

· CHAPTER 9 ·
CUTE AND CUDDLY NO MORE

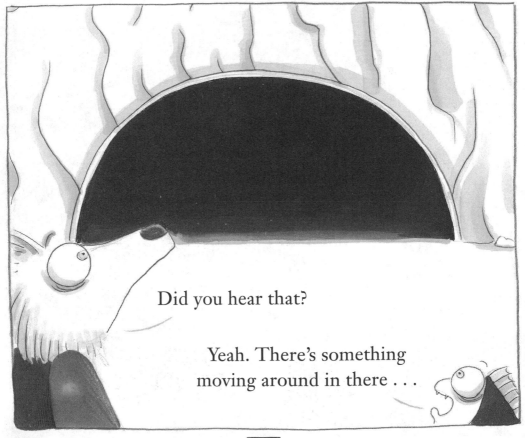

Did you hear that?

Yeah. There's something moving around in there . . .

Are you guys ready for this?

NO.

Fair enough.
I'm not sure I am either.
But it doesn't matter,
does it? Because we have
a job to do. It's up to us
to protect the world.

It's up to us—
**THE GOOD
GUYS CLUB.**

Seriously, man, now that we've heard about the **INTERNATIONAL LEAGUE OF HEROES**, our name sounds so lame it makes me wish I had hands—so I could **SLAP YOU**.

Really? You don't like our name?

IT SUCKS.

OK . . . well . . . We **ARE** helping the awesome League of Heroes, right now . . .

So that kind of makes us awesome, too, doesn't it?

Kind of.

Well then, Kind-of-Awesome-League-of-Good-Guys-Guys, let's show this SECRET WEAPON what we're made of!

Hey! **HAHAHAHA!**
Everybody relax!
LOOK!
IT'S JUST ANOTHER **TRICK!**
IT'S JUST A BUNCH OF . . .

Phew!
Well, **THAT'S** a relief!

No, no, no . . . wait a minute . . .
There's something **WEIRD**
about those kittens.
Why are they **LIMPING?**
And **MOANING?**
And . . . **DROOLING?**

NO!
IT CAN'T BE!
IT IS!
IT'S . . .
IT'S AN ARMY
OF . . .

ZOMBIE KITTENS!

It's a ZOMBIE KITTEN APOCALYPSE!

Should you **panic**? Should you **cry**?

Should you **poop your pants**?

NO! You should sit back and watch the **FUR FLY** as the world's **BADDEST GOOD GUYS** take on **MAD MARMALADE'S MEOWING MONSTERS!**

You'll **laugh till you cry**. Or **laugh till you fart**. (It doesn't matter which, it's totally your choice.)

Just don't miss . . . the **BAD GUYS** in *Attack of the Zittens*.

31901060933571